Life with Mammoth

By
Ian Fraser

Illustrated by
Mary Ann Fraser

Marshall Cavendish Children

Marshall Cavendish Corporation, 99 White Plains Road,

Tarrytown, NY 10591 www.marshallcavendish.us/kids

Library of Congress Cataloging-in-Publication Data

Fraser, Ian (Ian Noel), 1989- Life with mammoth / Ian Fraser ; [illustrations by] Mary Ann Fraser.—1st ed. p. cm.—(Ogg and Bob) Summary: Cavemen Ogg and Bob search for their "pet" mammoth, Mug, to give him a bath, then try to figure out which of them is Mug's best friend. ISBN 978-0-7614-5722-0 [1. Prehistoric peoples—Fiction. 2. Mammoths—Fiction. 3. Wild animals as pets—Fiction. 4. Youths' writings.] I. Fraser, Mary Ann, ill. II. Title. PZ7.F86434Lif 2010 [E]—dc22

2009029030

The illustrations were rendered in ink and gouache on paper.

Book design by Vera Soki   Editor: Marilyn Brigham

Printed in Malaysia (T)

A Marshall Cavendish Chapter Book

First edition

1 3 5 6 4 2

mc **Marshall Cavendish**
Children

For Todd Carter Cook, my best friend
—I.F.

To Danielle, Timmy, and Jonny
—M.F.

Contents

Meet the Characters

This is Ogg. He lives in a cave with his best friend, Bob, and his pet mammoth, Mug. Ogg is good at thinking of things to do. Ogg doesn't like baths. He likes rocks and food, but most of all he loves to play with Bob and Mug.

This is Bob. Bob lives in a cave with his best friend, Ogg, and his pet mammoth, Mug. He is good at solving the problems that he and Ogg encounter. Bob doesn't like bugs or being eaten by saber-tooth tigers. He likes thinking and exploring with Ogg and Mug.

This is Mug. Mug is Ogg and Bob's large, hairy pet mammoth. He is good at causing problems. Mug likes to eat, sleep, and play games.

This is Saber-tooth Tiger. He is good at hunting. Saber-tooth Tiger likes to eat mammoths and cavemen with his two big teeth. This is a problem for Ogg, Bob, and Mug.

Chapter 1
Bath Time

"Bob? What that smell?" asked Ogg.

"Ogg's feet," said Bob.

"No, me wash feet ten days ago," said Ogg. "It Mug."

"Mug need bath," said Bob.

"Hey! Where Mug go?" cried Ogg.

"He hiding," said Bob. "Mug not like baths."

"How we find Mug?" asked Ogg.

"We need to think like mammoth," said Bob. "If me mammoth, me hide . . . in tree."

"No, silly, Mug not hide in tree. Mug afraid of heights," replied Ogg.

"Me look anyway," said Bob.

"See? No mammoth," said Ogg.

"Hmm," said Ogg. "If me mammoth, me hide . . . under rock."

"No, silly, Mug not hide under rock," Bob said. "Buggies under rock. BIG BUGGIES!"

"Me look anyway," said Ogg.

Ogg and Bob tried to lift the rock.
"Rock too heavy," said Ogg.

"Hmm," said Bob. "If me mammoth, me hide . . . in bush."

"Mug in bush!" Ogg agreed.

Ogg and Bob walked into the patch of bushes.

"Mug not in bush," Bob said.

"Mug is better hider than we are finders," said Ogg.

Suddenly it started to pour.

"If me mammoth," they said together, "me go back to cave."

Ogg and Bob hurried home.

"Look, we find Mug!" said Bob.

"Why Mug running around in rain?" asked Ogg.

"Mug not like bath," said Bob. "Mug like shower."

Chapter 2
Cave Art

It rained and rained. After dinner Ogg and Bob sat around their campfire.

Ogg looked around. "Cave boring. Need color!" he said.

Ogg picked up a stick from the fire. He started drawing on the wall.

Bob sat and watched. "What you drawing?" asked Bob.

"Rock!" answered Ogg.

"Why draw rock?" asked Bob. "Cave already *is* rock. Me try!"

"What is that?" said Ogg.

"Tree!" said Bob.

"Why draw tree?" asked Ogg. "Tree not belong in cave!"

"What we draw then?" Bob asked.

Ogg scratched his head. Bob sat and thought.

"I know!" they both said. "We draw Mug!"

Ogg and Bob went to work. When they were done, they looked at their picture.

"Picture look funny," said Ogg.

"Picture too thin," said Bob. "Mug is fat."

Ogg nodded. "Mug very fat. We try again."

"Still not look right," said Bob.
"I know," said Ogg. "Mug also hairy!"

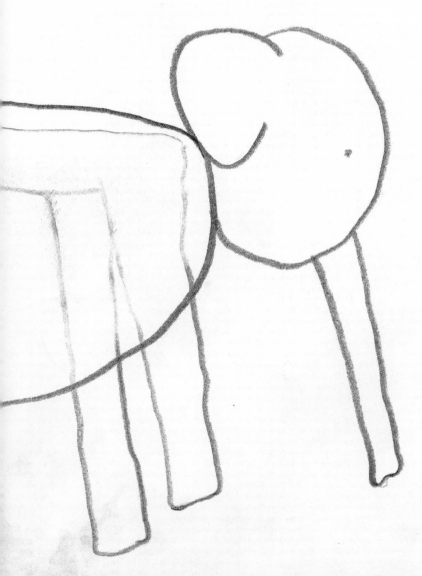

"Mug has hair all over," said Bob. "Now picture look more funny!"

"Not look like Mug," said Ogg, "Look like mess!"

Just then Mug came in from the rain.

"Mug all muddy," shouted the cave-men. "Mug OUT."

Mug lumbered back out. Ogg and Bob
stared at the cave wall.

"Look, Mug make picture," said Ogg.

"Me add tail," said Ogg.

"Me add tusks," said Bob.

They stood back and looked at the drawing.

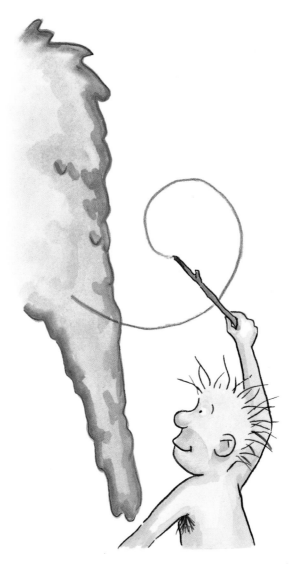

"Something missing," said Ogg.

"I know!" said Bob. "*We* missing!"

Ogg and Bob ran outside and rolled in the mud.

Then Ogg and Bob came back inside. They splattered themselves on the cave wall.

"Cave not boring anymore!" said Ogg and Bob.

Chapter 3
Best Friend

Bob felt something poking him. He rolled over and saw Mug's trunk.

"Mug, go back to sleep," said Ogg.

"Mug hungry," said Bob. "I give Mug food. I Mug's best friend."

"No!" said Ogg, jumping up. "*I* Mug's best friend! I do it."

"Why *you* Mug's best friend?" asked Bob.

"I always bring Mug his favorite food," replied Ogg.

"No, you don't," said Bob.

"I do, too!" said Ogg. "Mug just doesn't eat it."

"Nobody eats rocks, Ogg," said Bob.

"Well, why *you* Mug's best friend then?" asked Ogg as they went outside.

"I play fetch with Mug," said Bob. "Watch."

Bob threw a stick. Mug ran off.

Mug came back with a tree.

"See, Mug like me better!" said Bob. "I throw stick, Mug bring back tree!"

"I can do better. I show you," said Ogg.

Ogg tied a vine to Mug's tusk. Ogg started walking. Mug followed along behind him.

"See! I take Mug for walk," Ogg said.

Suddenly Mug started running.

"No, Ogg, Mug take *you* for walk!"
said Bob, running after them.

Soon Mug got thirsty and stopped to drink at the river. Ogg and Bob rested on the shore.

Mug looked up. A saber-tooth tiger was staring at them from across the river.

"Look! Kitty!" said Ogg.

"Uh-oh!" said Bob. "Kitty look hungry!"

Ogg, Bob, and Mug turned and ran.
The saber-tooth tiger chased them all the
way back to the cave.

Ogg and Bob took burning sticks from the fire and waved them to scare off the saber-tooth tiger.

"Being Mug's friend is hard work," said Ogg.

Bob nodded. "But we still don't know who Mug's *best* friend is," he said.

"We need a plan," said Ogg.

"I have idea," said Bob. "You stand there. Me stand here. We call Mug. We see who Mug's best friend is."

"Okay," said Ogg.

"COME, Mug," they called together.

Mug came running. He ran right between them to the big pile of food.

"Awww," they sighed together. "Maybe food is Mug's best friend."

Ogg and Bob looked at each other.

"It okay, Bob," said Ogg. "You *my* best friend."

"You *my* best friend, too," said Bob.

"Let's eat," they said together.